CHAPPAQUA LIBRARY
CHAPPAQUA, NY

W9-BFA-304

Anna Grossnickle Hines

PIECES

A YEAR IN POEMS & QUILTS

Greenwillow Books
An Imprint of
HarperCollins *Publishers*

Pieces

Pieces of the seasons
appear and disappear
in a patchwork pattern
making up a year.

June '01

Chappaqua Library
Chappaqua, NY 10514

Ballet

Slow motion,
crow lands
on a cedar branch.
Branch bounces.
Crow dances.

In March

The long winter snow
melts in drips
and trickles
as, mittenless,
I splash in puddles,
squishing mud
on my boots,
while the creek
bubbles in celebration.

Just When I Thought

It was a great day for clouds
and I wanted to tell someone.
So I said it
a couple of times,
and just when I thought
no one was listening
a raindrop fell
on me.

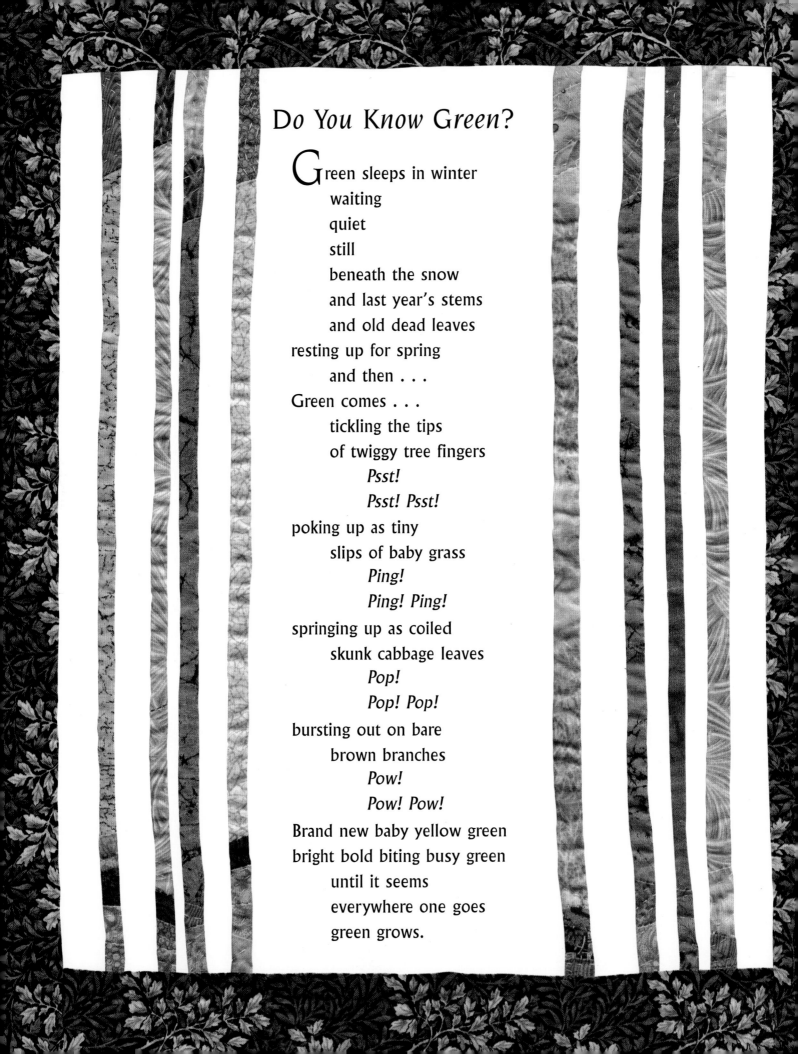

Do You Know Green?

Green sleeps in winter
    waiting
    quiet
    still
    beneath the snow
    and last year's stems
    and old dead leaves
resting up for spring
    and then . . .
Green comes . . .
    tickling the tips
    of twiggy tree fingers
        Psst!
        Psst! Psst!
poking up as tiny
    slips of baby grass
        Ping!
        Ping! Ping!
springing up as coiled
    skunk cabbage leaves
        Pop!
        Pop! Pop!
bursting out on bare
    brown branches
        Pow!
        Pow! Pow!
Brand new baby yellow green
bright bold biting busy green
    until it seems
    everywhere one goes
    green grows.

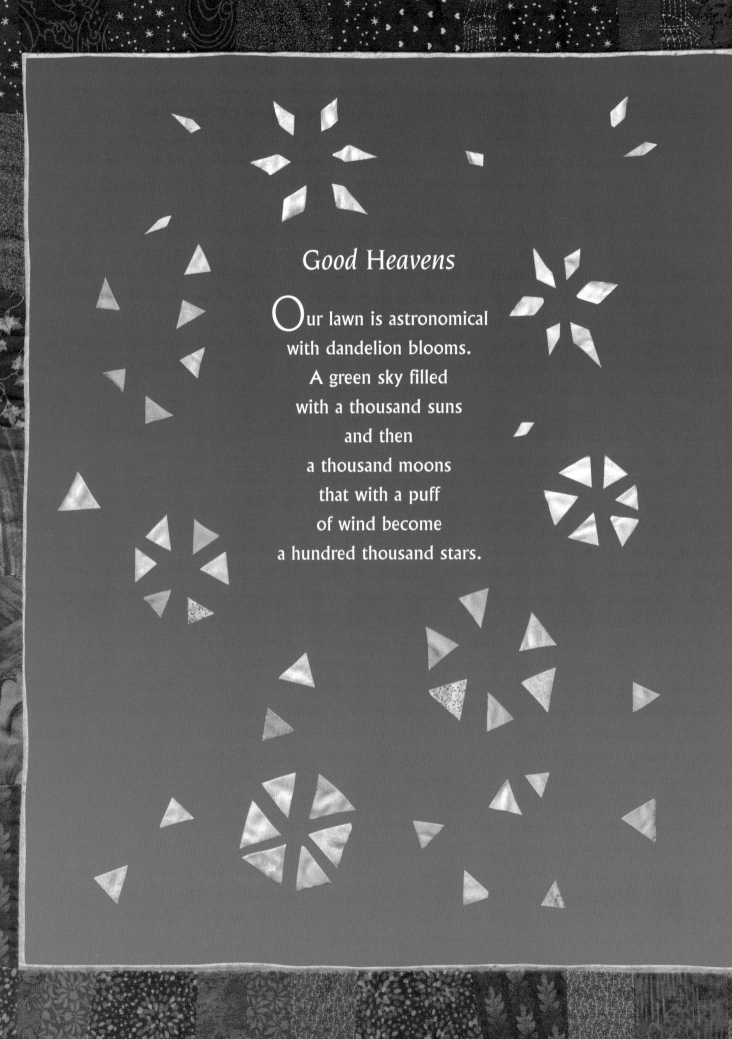

Good Heavens

Our lawn is astronomical
with dandelion blooms.
A green sky filled
with a thousand suns
and then
a thousand moons
that with a puff
of wind become
a hundred thousand stars.

Nose Knows

Locusts line the walkway,
lilacs by the wall,
lily of the valley,
the sweetest smell of all.

Put me in a blindfold
so I can't see a thing.
Even with my eyes closed
I'll still know it's spring.

Mirage

Oh, phlox, I like
the way you make
the garden floor
a purple lake.

Takeout

Papa Wren stops
on the rock
beneath
the rosebush,
tasty tidbit in his beak.
Looks
   this way . . .
   that way . . .
      slips
      behind the ferns
      to the nest
      where Mama sits
      warming eggs
      and waiting
      for Papa's tasty bits.

*En*core

A hummingbird is
darting
   zip zip
      flitting
   zip zip
dipping
   sip sip
    sucking
   scarlet sweetness
    from the trumpets
  on the
honeysuckle vine.

Misplaced?

In a mass of wild confusion
flowers bloom in great profusion,
brilliant dazzling bold infusion,
pink-blue purple stimulation,
red-gold-yellow conflagration,
rousing raucous celebration,
stirring us to jubilation,
echoing the exultation
of their bright and vibrant show!
But, I am curious to know,
since bloomers are not sleepyheads,
why do they grow in flower beds?

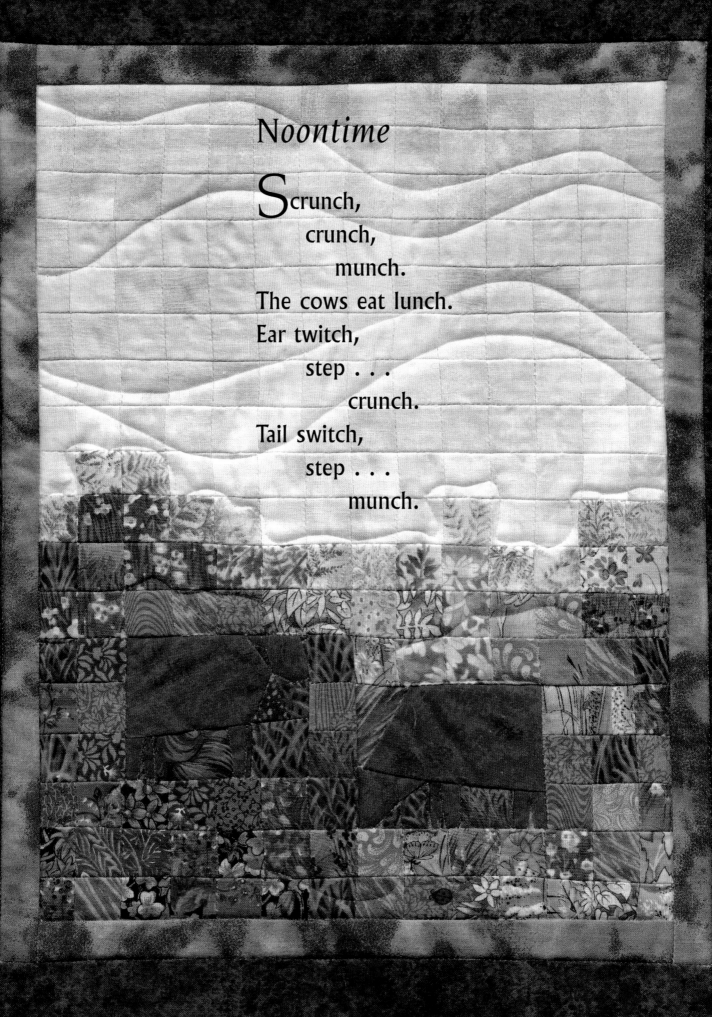

Noontime

Scrunch,
  crunch,
    munch.
The cows eat lunch.
Ear twitch,
    step . . .
      crunch.
Tail switch,
    step . . .
      munch.

Rock and Roll

Jitterbug, swing, or boogie-woogie,
Tango, twist, and hokeypokey.
Every time there is a breeze,
The leaves are dancing in the trees.

To Each His Own

When the leaves fall
  some float
      lazily
        wavily
  and taking all
          daysily
              drift
  to the ground.
Some flutter
        skuttering
              whuttering
  audibly uttering
              whispers
                  of sound.
When the leaves fall
  some
      come in bunches
                swirling
          and whirling
            twisting
      and twirling
              round
                  about
                  round.
Some
    skip-a-dip
        bippity
            floppity
                flippity
            toppity
          tippity
    plippity
        down.
And some
    just drop
      flop.

Pageantry

The trees are wearing
scarlet gowns
and golden crowns
and bits of them
are falling down.

Ode to a Rake

In the wind
the leaves fall
　　floating
　　　fluttering
pretty as snowflakes

except . . .
they don't melt.

Silhouettes

In light bark
and dark bark
the trees stand
bare-boned
naked
against
the winter sky.

Shadows

Do you know what the trees
are doing in the winter
with their branches reaching
    up and out
    and all about
making crisscross shadows
little twiggy spriggy shadows
long lanky liney shadows
    all around?

They're sunbathing.

Winter Sunshine

Today it is December.
Time for winter weather
and the air is frosty chilly,
only . . .
No one told the rosebush
and it has two yellow blossoms,
two spots of sunshine
to warm away the cold.

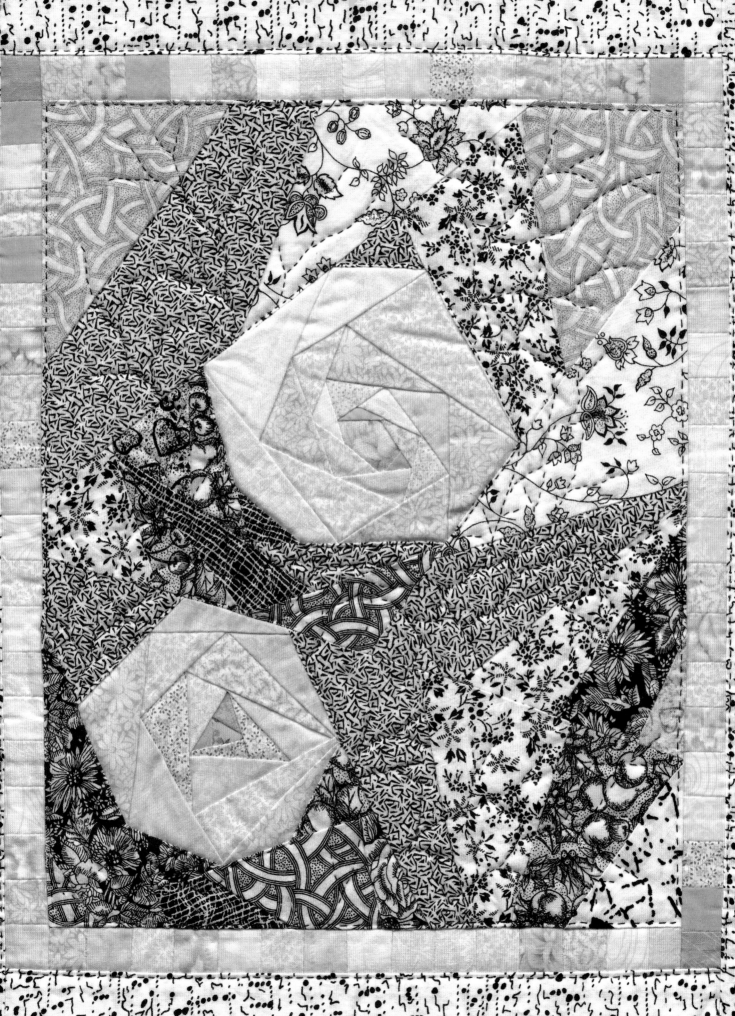

Magic Show

Sometimes in winter
while I'm sleeping
through the night
inside the house
all snug and tight,
outside
the world is turning
white.

Each of the squares in this quilt that my mother is sitting on was made by one of her siblings, children, grandchildren, or friends. This is the project that got me started.

The Story Behind the Quilts

It's all my mother's fault. First, when I was a child, she told me that I should do whatever I wanted to do. Then she started making beautiful quilts.

When the family decided to make a quilt secretly for Mom, I wanted to make several squares for it. I looked through Mom's books and magazines for ideas and asked her lots of questions. To keep her from being suspicious, I told her I was thinking of illustrating a book with quilts. Actually that idea had occurred to me before, but it seemed too crazy to say out loud until I had this chance to pretend that I didn't really mean it. Mom seemed a little surprised at first, but if that was what I wanted to do, she was more than willing to help. She collected fabric scraps from her friends and brought out more books for me to look at. Maybe it wasn't such a crazy idea.

I'd made quilts for each of my children—big, simple designs using large pieces of fabric. I'd sewn their clothing and enough dolls and stuffed animals to fill a well-stocked toy store, and now the squares for my mother's quilt, but I'd never done anything as intricate as the quilts I was visualizing for my book. Could I really do it?

In 1996, at my mother's dining room table, I drew the design for "Good Heavens," spread out the blue, green, yellow, and white fabrics, and began to sew. Sewing pieces of fabric together in a design is called *piecing*. Strip by strip I sewed the tiny bits of fabric together until the whole thing was pieced. Golden suns and white moons and stars floated from the green lawn to the deep blue sky. It worked! I could do it!

Over the next three years I purchased hundreds of strips and squares of fabric and made eighteen more designs. I used piecing for "Ballet" and "Do You Know Green?" The winter tree pair ("Silhouettes" and "Shadows") I pieced using very small squares of fabric. Then I appliquéd the branches. To *appliqué* is to sew smaller pieces of fabric on top of a larger piece to make a picture or a decorative design. "Take Out" is done completely with appliqué. Appliqué can be done with a sewing machine, but I did mine by hand, turning the edges under with the needle as I went.

The next step was to quilt the designs. This is done by sandwiching a layer of cotton padding between the design and a piece of backing fabric and then stitching a decorative pattern through all the layers. *Quilting* is the stitching, and it can be done by hand or machine. Fine hand quilting is admired for tiny, even stitches. "Take Out" and "Ballet" were two of the first designs I quilted by hand. The winter trees pages were my first efforts at machine quilting.

My mother told me that quilting is contagious, and she is right. She was inspired to start by her sister. The two of them, along with two sisters-in-law and a brother, come from three corners of the country to meet at quilt shows, visit fabric stores, and share ideas. I have visited my mother's quilt guild in Santa Clarita, California, and joined the local Milford Valley Quilters Guild in Pennsylvania, where I've found even more support and encouragement.

In addition to using donated scraps, I purchased more than three hundred pieces of fabric and organized them by color.

Many of the designs were pieced using 1 1/8-inch squares. I cut thousands of squares!

Working with such small pieces, it is important to be very precise. Often I had to take out seams because they were just a tiny bit off, or because I had sewn the wrong edges together or changed my mind about a particular color in a particular spot. Many seams were sewn two or three times, especially on more complex designs like "Pieces."

Some of the pictures were pieced by sewing the fabric onto a paper backing. This is the design for one of the cows.

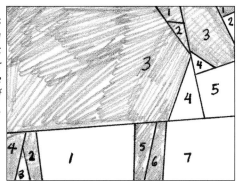

After sewing the cows, I arranged them with the squares on a sheet of foam and began sewing all the pieces together, strip by strip.

The seam takes up 1/4 inch of each side of each square, so each square ends up being just 5/8 of an inch. It is always surprising to see how much the design shrinks when it is sewn. Each of the finished quilts is approximately 12 by 18 inches.

On the back you can see the fabric that gets hidden by the seams. You can also see the paper backing I used to make the cows. This was torn away before the design was quilted.

For machine quilting I often draw the design on a piece of tracing paper to guide my stitching. Here I am quilting one of the autumn leaf designs.

My mother is hand quilting one of her bed-sized quilts. She is using a hoop to hold the layers of fabric and batting (the padding) in place as she makes her fine, even stitches.

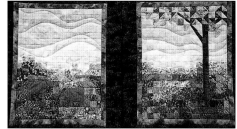

These quilting lines add dimension to the cows, tree, and horizon, and add a feeling of air moving in the sky.

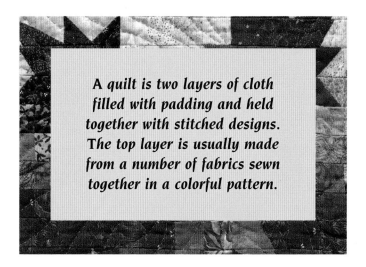

A quilt is two layers of cloth filled with padding and held together with stitched designs. The top layer is usually made from a number of fabrics sewn together in a colorful pattern.

Quilting is an age-old American tradition, an art form, a means of self-expression, a way of using scraps and parts of worn clothing to provide warm and attractive bedcovers. But it is more than that. It provides a way for people to connect with one another to share a common passion and a wonderful heritage.

Information on quilting can be found in many books and magazines, but Mom (Ruth Grossnickle to the rest of the world) and I recommend finding a quilter to talk to or taking a class. On the Internet, the World Wide Quilting Page has lists of guilds, quilt stores, shows, exhibits and museums, chatrooms, and lots of how-to tips [http://www.quilt.com/MainQuiltingPage.html].

Selected Bibliography

Cleland, Lee. *Quilting Makes the Quilt*. Bothell, Wash.: That Patchwork Place, Inc., 1994.

Magaret, Patricia Maixner, and Donna Ingram Slusser. *Watercolor Quilts*. Bothell, Wash.: That Patchwork Place, Inc., 1993.

——.*Watercolor Impressions*. Bothell, Wash.: That Patchwork Place, Inc., 1995.

McDowell, Ruth B. *Piecing: Expanding the Basics*. Lafayette, Ca.: C & T Publishing, 1998.

Wolfrom, Joen. *Landscapes and Illusions: Creating Scenic Imagery with Fabric*. Lafayette, Ca.: C & T Publishing, 1990.

The Foundation Piecer, a pattern journal published by Zippy Designs Publishing, Newport, VA.

For my mother, who told me, "If that's what you want to do, that's what you should do."

With thanks also to the other family quilters: Aunt Esther, Aunt Frances, Aunt Betty, and adjunct quilter Uncle Bob; and to my mother's friends in the Santa Clarita Valley Quilt Guild, all of whom offered support and sent scraps to help me get started.

The handmade quilts used as illustrations in this book were reproduced in full color. The original quilts are approximately the same size as printed. For more information please turn to the two previous pages. The photographs on those pages were taken by Gary Hines.

The text type is Flareserif 821.

Pieces
Copyright © 2001 by Anna Grossnickle Hines
All rights reserved.
Printed in Hong Kong
by South China Printing Company (1988) Ltd.
www.harperchildrens.com

The poem "Just When I Thought,"
copyright © 1992 by Anna Grossnickle Hines,
first appeared in *Weather Reports*, edited
by Jane Yolen, published in 1993
by Wordsong/Boyds Mills Press.

The poem "Good Heavens,"
copyright © 1994 by Anna Grossnickle Hines,
was first published in the July 1994 issue of *Cricket*.

Library of Congress Cataloging-in-Publication Data
Hines, Anna Grossnickle.
Pieces: a year in poems and quilts /
by Anna Grossnickle Hines.
    p. cm.
"Greenwillow Books."
Summary: Poems about the four seasons,
as reflected in the natural world, are
accompanied by photographs of quilts
made by the author.
ISBN 0-688-16963-5 (trade).
ISBN 0-688-16964-3 (lib. bdg.)
1. Nature—Juvenile poetry. 2. Seasons—Juvenile poetry.
3. Children's poetry, American. 4. Quilts—Pictorial
works—Juvenile literature.
[1. Nature—Poetry. 2. Seasons—Poetry.
3. American poetry. 4. Quilts.] I. Title.
PS3558.I528 P54 2001
811'.54—dc21   99-086463

2 3 4 5 6 7 8 9 10
First Edition

J 811.5 H
Hines, Anna Grossnickle
Pieces

J 811.5 H
Hines, Anna Grossnickle
Pieces